I Am a Princess

By Andrea Posner-Sanchez

Illustrated by
Francesco Legramandi
and Gabriella Matta

A GOLDEN BOOK • NEW YORK

randomhouse.com/kids ISBN: 978-0-7364-2906-1 Printed in the United States of America

10 9 8 7 6 5 4 3 2 1

Hello! My name is Cinderella. I am a princess.

I live in a beautiful castle and have lots of fancy gowns and jewels. But not all princesses are the same—we each enjoy doing our own special thing.

I love caring for animals . . .

. . . and having them care for me!

I am Ariel.

I love to sing. Sometimes my sisters and
I perform concerts for our father, King Triton.

I also love to collect treasures from the human world. This statue of Prince Eric is my favorite!

Hello! I am Snow White.

I like to have fun with my friends Happy, Sleepy, Sneezy, Grumpy, Doc, Bashful, and Dopey . . .

. . . and then surprise them with a sweet treat.

My name is Tiana, and I love to cook!

Even when I was a frog, I made a tasty gumbo for my friends Prince Naveen, Louis, and Ray.

Now I get to make lots of people happy with my food—at my very own restaurant!

Hello! I am Rapunzel.

I love to paint pictures . . .

. . . and play with Pascal.
He is really good at hide-and-seek!

My name is Aurora.

When I was a baby, I was given the gift of song, so I love music.

Now I enjoy dancing with Prince Phillip whenever we get the chance!

My name is Jasmine.

I love going on adventures with Aladdin beside me!

Bonjour! I am Belle.

I love to read all kinds of books.

I even like to read about other princesses. Don't you?